Freeze, Goldilocks!

by Feana Tu'akoi

illustrated by Fraser Williamson

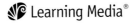
Learning Media®

Scenes

Characters

MOTHER BEAR

FATHER BEAR

BABY BEAR

GOLDILOCKS

SERGEANT

OFFICER

Here are some ideas to help you set up the stage.

Scene 1
OUTSIDE THE THREE BEARS' HOUSE

*The **THREE BEARS** walk onstage and stop suddenly.*

FATHER BEAR: Did you leave that door open?

MOTHER BEAR: No. I thought I'd locked it.

BABY BEAR: You did lock it! I saw you.

FATHER BEAR: Then I don't think we should go inside yet.

MOTHER BEAR: You're right. We'd better call the police.

> **FATHER BEAR** *takes out his cell phone.*

SERGEANT (*picking up the phone*):
Good morning. Downtown Police
Station. How can I help you?

FATHER BEAR: Hello. There's been a
break-in at seven Honeybee Lane.
We locked the door when we went
out, but when we came back, it was
wide open.

SERGEANT: Was there any porridge in the house?

FATHER BEAR: Yes, there was. I made porridge for breakfast, but it was too hot, so we left it and went out for a walk. How did you know?

SERGEANT: Try not to panic, sir, but I think this could be the work of a kid called Goldilocks.

FATHER BEAR: Goldilocks? I've seen that name spray-painted on walls around town.

SERGEANT: That's her tag, all right. She's been on a crime spree lately — breaking and entering, stealing food, and vandalizing furniture. She doesn't usually hurt people, but you should stay where you are until we get there, just in case.

FATHER BEAR: OK, then. We'll wait for you here. Good-bye.

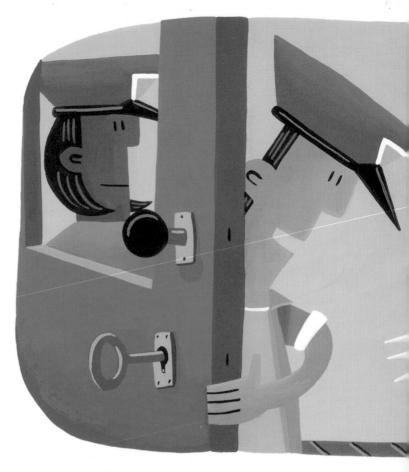

The **POLICE OFFICERS** *walk across*
the stage to the **THREE BEARS**.

SERGEANT: Any sign of her?

MOTHER BEAR: None at all. It's been
very quiet.

SERGEANT: She's probably gone by now, but we'll go in first, just in case.

OFFICER: Everybody follow me.

Scene 2
IN THE THREE BEARS' KITCHEN

The **THREE BEARS** *follow the* **POLICE OFFICERS** *over to the table.*

SERGEANT: Have a good look around. Is everything how you left it?

FATHER BEAR (*shaking his head and pointing*): Somebody's been eating my porridge.

MOTHER BEAR: Oh, no! Somebody's been eating *my* porridge.

BABY BEAR: And somebody's been eating my porridge, and they've eaten it all up!

OFFICER (*bending over to pick up a hair*): Aha! Look at this – a piece of golden, curly hair.

SERGEANT: Just as I thought – Goldilocks!

> *The* **OFFICER** *puts the hair into a plastic bag.*

SERGEANT: We'll go and look in the living room next. The place might be a little messed up, so walk carefully, just in case.

OFFICER: Everybody follow me.

Scene 3
IN THE THREE BEARS' LIVING ROOM

The **THREE BEARS** *follow the*
POLICE OFFICERS *over to the chairs.*

FATHER BEAR (*pointing*): Somebody's
been sitting in my chair.

MOTHER BEAR: Oh, no! Somebody's
been sitting in *my* chair.

BABY BEAR: And somebody's been sitting in my chair, and they've broken it all up!

SERGEANT: Well, that's it. It's Goldilocks's M.O. all right.

BABY BEAR: What's an M.O.?

OFFICER: It's short for modus operandi. It means that this is what she usually does when she's committing a crime. First she eats the porridge, and then she sits on all the chairs.

BABY BEAR: What does she do next?

OFFICER: Er … I can't remember.
Do you know, sarge?

SERGEANT: Hmmm … It was
something to do with the bedroom,
but I'm not sure what.

MOTHER BEAR: We'd better go and
take a look, then.

SERGEANT: Let the officer lead the way, just in case.

OFFICER: Everybody follow me.

Scene 4
IN THE THREE BEARS' BEDROOM

The **THREE BEARS** *follow the* **POLICE OFFICERS** *to the beds.*

FATHER BEAR: Somebody's been sleeping in my bed.

MOTHER BEAR: Oh, no! Somebody's been sleeping in *my* bed.

BABY BEAR (*pointing*): And somebody's been sleeping in my bed, and she's still there!

GOLDILOCKS *sits up in bed and rubs her eyes.*

GOLDILOCKS: Oh, no – it's the cops!

SERGEANT *and* **OFFICER** *(together)*: Freeze, Goldilocks!

GOLDILOCKS: I'm getting out of here!

MOTHER BEAR: Look out! She's going to jump out the window!

GOLDILOCKS: Here I go ... Aargh!

GOLDILOCKS *jumps off the bed and runs offstage.*

BABY BEAR: Cool! Can I jump, too?

OFFICER: After her! Follow me!

> **POLICE OFFICERS** *and* **FATHER BEAR** *run after* **GOLDILOCKS** *then come back onstage, puffing.* **GOLDILOCKS** *stays offstage.*

Scene 5
INSIDE THE THREE BEARS' HOUSE

OFFICER: Oh, no! She got away from us again!

SERGEANT: Don't worry – we'll get her next time. Father Bear, I think you should get a stronger lock on your door, just in case.

FATHER BEAR: Good idea.

SERGEANT: Goldilocks isn't the only crook out there, you know. There's a really sneaky one called the Big Bad Wolf. He knocks on the door and pretends to be someone you know.

OFFICER: And if that doesn't work, he yells, "Let me come in, or I'll huff, and I'll puff, and I'll blow your house in!" He means it, too! Just last week, he made three little pigs move out of their houses. He's a big bully.

FATHER BEAR: We'll be very careful from now on. Thanks for your help, officers.

SERGEANT: No problem. We have to go now. They need us back at the station.

OFFICER: Call us if you have any more trouble. So long.

The **THREE BEARS** *wave as the* **POLICE OFFICERS** *leave.*

There is a knocking sound from offstage.

MOTHER BEAR (*looking at* **FATHER BEAR**): Who's there?

WOLF VOICE: Little pig ... oops! I mean ... little bear, little bear, let me come in!

FATHER BEAR (*taking out his cell phone*):
Oh, no! Here we go again!